TWO
BY
TWO

The Untold Story

TWO
BY
TWO

The Untold Story

KATHRYN HEWITT

Harcourt Brace Jovanovich, Publishers

San Diego   New York   London

To my son, Paul

HBJ

Requests for permission to make copies of any part of the work should
be mailed to: Permissions, Harcourt Brace Jovanovich, Publishers,
Orlando, Florida 32887

Library of Congress Cataloging in Publication Data
Hewitt, Kathryn.
Two by two.
Summary: In order to convince his family and all the
animals to come aboard the Ark, Noah sends out invitations
announcing a romantic vacation cruise.
1. Noah (Biblical figure) — Juvenile fiction. 2. Noah's
ark — Juvenile fiction. [1. Noah (Biblical figure) —
Fiction. 2. Noah's ark — Fiction. 3. Animals — Fiction.
4. Ships — Fiction] I. Title.
PZ7.H4493Tw 1984   [E]   84-4579
ISBN 0-15-291801-9

Designed by Dalia Hartman

Printed in the United States of America

First edition   A B C D E

Long ago, in a faraway land, the people forgot how
to get along together. Only Noah and his family
remembered how to be happy.

Maybe that's why God remembered to tell Noah about the flood that was coming.

God sent a messenger with a plan. "Two by two," the messenger kept saying. "Two by two."

Noah ran to tell his wife and sons and daughters about
the flood and about the plan.

"A flood!" hooted his sons.

"Two by two!" giggled his daughters.

"No jokes, Noah," sighed his wife. "I don't have time."

Noah went ahead with the messenger's plan, anyway. He began building an ark that would carry all the animals, two by two, for as long as the flood lasted.

Noah worried as he worked. "How am I going to get the animals to go aboard?" he asked himself. "If my own family won't listen, how will I make the beasts believe me?"

Then the idea came to Noah. "I've got it!" he shouted. "I'll make the trip a pleasure cruise! Fun and games and fresh sea air! We'll travel in style. How can the animals say no to that?"

Noah sent invitations to all the animals.
FORTY DAYS AND NIGHTS OF ROMANCE AND ADVENTURE,
the invitations read. A SPECIAL TIME FOR THE TWO OF YOU.

"On a deluxe vessel, too!" the animals whooped to their mates. "Well, when it rains, it pours!"

While Noah hurried to finish his ark

. . . animals everywhere were packing for their cruise.
"Now, don't forget the film!" was heard throughout the land.

Soon it was time to leave. From zebra to bear to lion, all the animals came. From elephant to kangaroo to cat, they all came two by two.

Noah was there to greet the animals.
Noah's family was there to help.
"Bon voyage!" they said.

No one seemed to notice the rain beginning as the ark
left the shore. Everyone was having much too fine a time.
    "We haven't taken a vacation in *years*!" many
animals told each other.

But when it started raining harder, everyone had to go inside. That's when the problems began.

Some of the animals couldn't get into their cabins one by one, let alone two by two.

The wind and rain made the ark rock and sway.

Noah's wife and daughters and sons locked themselves in their cabins. Noah was left to serve dinner all alone.

"We want our dinner *now*!" growled the bears.

"I don't feel very hungry," moaned an elephant.

The rain kept raining.
"Will it never end?" a pig squealed.
"Whose idea was this?" a fox groused.
All around the ark, the animals pouted and fought.
You know how rainy days are.

And forty rainy days are forty times worse.

Noah tried parties and games and even a talent show. Nothing worked. Everyone was forgetting how to get along together.

"We have to remember how to be happy!" Noah pleaded.
"Otherwise, things will be as bad as they were back home."
Nobody wanted that. "We'll try," the animals promised.
"Then everybody dance!" Noah said. "Two by two."

Soon the room was filled with dancing couples. Noah sighed and smiled. A ray of sunlight touched his nose.

The clouds rolled away, and the animals grabbed
sunglasses and beach towels. The sun was out, at last!
It took many more days for the flood waters to
leave the land, but the animals didn't mind.

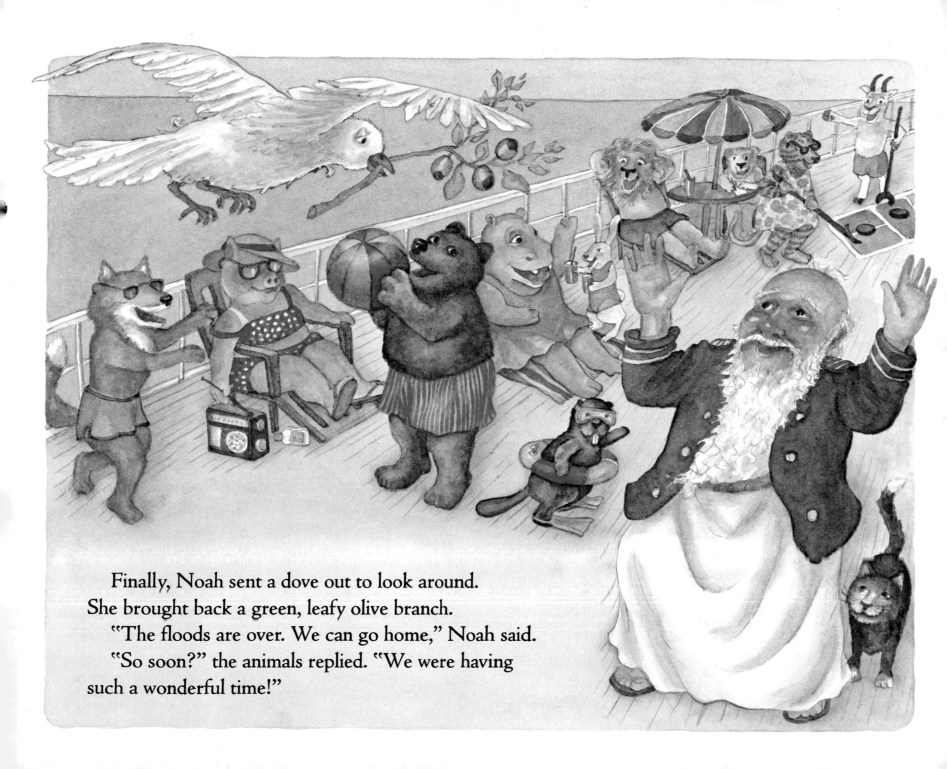

Finally, Noah sent a dove out to look around.
She brought back a green, leafy olive branch.
"The floods are over. We can go home," Noah said.
"So soon?" the animals replied. "We were having
such a wonderful time!"

But they did go home, marching off the ark two by two.
They thanked Noah warmly for the lovely vacation. And they
thanked him for reminding them how to be happy together.

And they never forgot again.